# YOU AND ME
# MURRAWEE

WRITTEN BY KERRI HASHMI

ILLUSTRATED BY FELICITY MARSHALL

PUFFIN BOOKS

We walk this same brown earth –
you and me, Murrawee.

Past the ancient granite rocks, we run down the slope to the river,
hearts beating in time. I follow your bare footsteps.

We move the same dust and bend the same grass in our stride.

The water is sparkling in the sun and it calls us near.

You've made a mud slide down the bank.
You sit on it and squeal as you slip with the other children
into the cold, clear water.

Your uncle is fishing upstream and
he warns you not to frighten the fish.

I give the slippery dip a miss,

take my shoes off and paddle near the edge.

The mud is squidgy between my toes.

My father calls to me to watch out for broken glass.

We each pick up a stick and draw pictures

in the same patch of river sand –

you and me, Murrawee.

You draw a kangaroo – mine is meant to be a horse.

We walk along the river bank, balance our way over the rocks, and scratch at the lichen.

I follow the footprints of someone's dog.

You think you've seen wallaby spoor.

Our fathers are going out in their boats. They leave from the
same little launching bay where the river bank is low.
My father has a row boat. He's teaching my brother
how to handle the oars.

Your father has a canoe.

He's taking your brother to show him how to trap fish.

We both watch them from the same spot on the shore,

in the shade of the old river red gum.

We can see the scars on it where your father cut his canoe.

The ducks on the river expect food from campers.

They swim up to me and I throw them some bread.

You know where their nest is. You swim across into the reeds to collect some eggs, which you give to your mother. She passes you her digging stick and asks you to gather some of the reed roots too. She'll cook them all tonight.

We climb up the path above the river – you and me, Murrawee.
The magpies are nesting too. They swoop on us and
we both run, ducking. The river water you are carrying
splashes from your coolamon.

A cool breeze is picking up and it blows our hair in our faces.

It brings the scent of food and the smoke of campfires.

Our tummies rumble. I can smell sausages and onions frying.

For you, the fish, the eggs and roots are baking.

We share food with our families.

The ants clean the crumbs and take them back to their nest,

as they have always done.

As we nestle in by the campfires in the dark, your grandmother takes you into her arms and tells you the old, old stories of the river, its creation, its floods and its droughts.

I strain to hear her stories, but they are lost in the winds of
time. Instead I listen with my family to songs on the radio,
sung by people who have never seen this river.

We lie down in the same hollow in the sand –

you and me, Murrawee.

The night is cool.

You lie between two fires and I snuggle into my sleeping-bag.

You hear the bunyip calling from the river.

The people in the next tent keep me awake for a while.

The moon shines on both our faces.
We sleep under the same stars, unchanged yet ever changing,
which spark like campfires in the sky.

We breathe the same air – you and me, Murrawee.

But we will never meet,

for we live two hundred years apart.

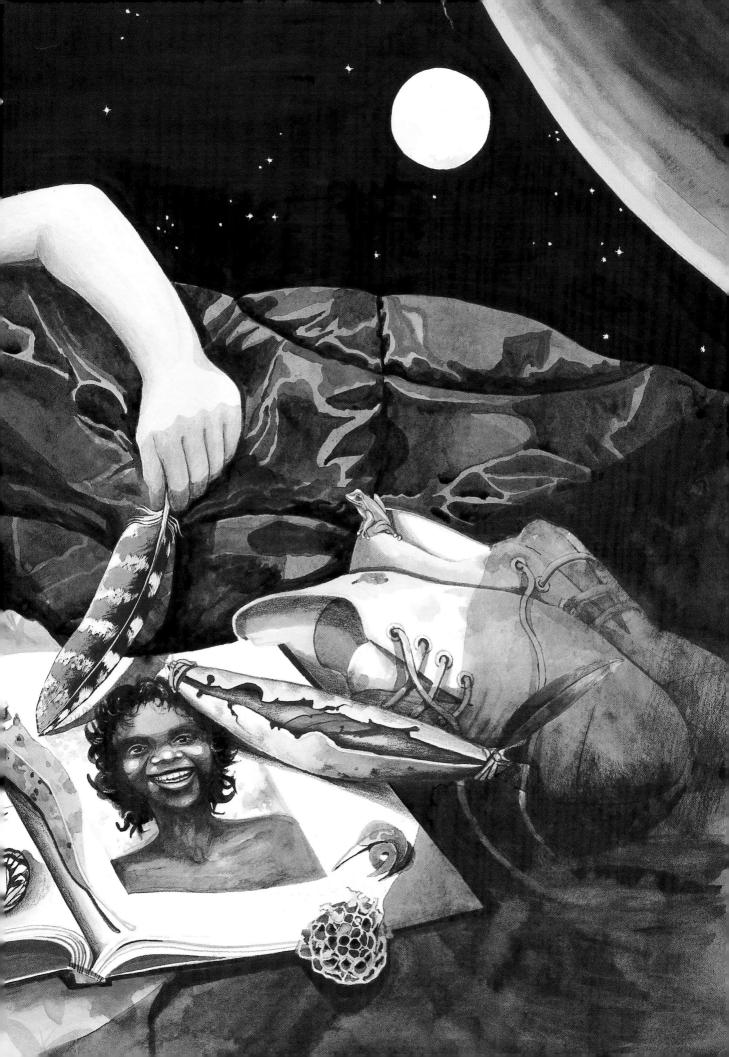

*To Omar and Natasha – K.H.*

*To Kate and Leo – F.M.*

The paintings in this book were created using watercolour, gouache and coloured pencil.

'Murrawee' means 'elder sister' in the language of the Ngarrindjeri people from the Murray River in South Australia. The author gratefully acknowledges the assistance of Stephanie Gollan, a Ngarrindjeri speaker from Taoundi Inc., the Aboriginal Community College in Port Adelaide, in finding this word. The spelling is phonetic as the language is oral and there is no correct spelling as such.

The illustrator gratefully acknowledges the assistance of Alan West, former director of the Aboriginal Arts Board (Australia Council) and former Curator in Anthropology at the Museum of Victoria and Mark Grist, Curator South-Eastern Australia Dept. of Indigenous Studies, Museum of Victoria, in researching the artwork. Permission has been obtained from Des Morgan of the Yorta Yorta people to portray one of their traditional possum cloaks as shown in the illustration on pages 24 and 25.

Puffin Books
Penguin Books Australia Ltd, 487 Maroondah Highway, PO Box 257, Ringwood, Victoria 3134, Australia
Penguin Books Ltd, Harmondsworth, Middlesex, England
Penguin Putnam Inc., 375 Hudson Street, New York, New York 10014, USA
Penguin Books Canada Limited, 10 Alcorn Avenue, Toronto, Ontario, Canada M4V 3B2
Penguin Books (NZ) Ltd, Cnr Rosedale and Airborne Roads, Albany, Auckland, New Zealand
Penguin Books (South Africa) (Pty) Ltd, 5 Watkins Street, Denver Ext 4, 2094, South Africa
Penguin Books India (P) Ltd, 11, Community Centre, Panchsheel Park, New Delhi 110 017, India

First published by Penguin Books Australia, 1998
Published in Puffin, 1999

3 5 7 9 10 8 6 4 2

Text Copyright © Kerri Hashmi, 1998
Illustrations Copyright © Felicity Marshall, 1998

The moral right of the author and illustrator has been asserted

Designed by Cathy Larsen, Penguin Design Studio, Typeset in 18/30 pt Times New Roman
Made and printed in Hong Kong by South China Printing

National Library of Australia
Cataloguing-in-Publication data:

Hashmi, Kerri, 1955– .
You and me, Murrawee.

ISBN 0 14 056499 3.

I. Marshall, Felicity. II. Title.

A823.3

www.puffin.com.au.